# Charlie's Chill

by
Emmy Tidning

Applied Divination
Redmond

Published by Applied Divination
Edited by Emily Paper
Formatted for print by Applied Divination

This book is a work of fiction. If any part of Charlie's Chill resembles the life of a known person, living or dead, then they are and were very gifted, indeed.

First printing edition 2021
Applied Divination
www.applieddivination.com

# CHAPTER ONE

"Did you learn to drive at a monster truck rally?!"

Charlotte screamed at the driver of a large truck as he descended from the front cabin. From her shop's now-destroyed entryway, she stepped carefully but aggressively onto the sidewalk he'd so carelessly backed over and smashed to bits.

"I'm so sorry, ma'am," the driver took the last step down and surveyed the devastation he'd wrought. He'd backed up over Charlotte's once-beautiful glass and stone shop entrance. "This intersection is a strange one," he scratched his head.

Charlotte felt blood rush to her fists, "This intersection has existed for sixty frickin' years, asshole!"

The driver's smile weakened to shame. "I'm truly sorry," he repeated, cleaning his coke-bottle-thick glasses with his t-shirt, "I'm new to truck driving and I've never been to this town before."

"Everything okay, Dad?" A smooth voice called out from the cabin.

Charlotte looked up to the truck and her breath caught in her throat as she glimpsed dark, piercing eyes surveying the situation, and one arm in a haphazard sling.

"It's fine, Darius. You sit back. I've got this," the old man responded.

Darius moved out of view, a slight wince – painful but devastatingly handsome – flashed across his face as he sat back. Charlotte was sure she'd heard him groan, and she felt her heart leap out of her chest in concern.

She composed herself quickly and returned her attention to the truck driver. Her conscience reminded her that she'd just called him the A-word twice, an insult that was perhaps over the top. The driver was right, after all. The intersection was a strange one, with three small streets interconnecting at odd angles, and the entrance to her little shop jutting out from the smallest corner. She saw how easy it might be for a large moving truck to underestimate a turn and end up on the sidewalk, especially if the driver was new to town and couldn't see very well.

"Just-" Charlotte paused to take a breath, "-be careful in our little village, okay? We don't have a lot of shops left here, and mine isn't the only one with a sidewalk you can damage."

Charlotte's business partner, Faith, rounded the corner like militia on a mission. Not paying attention at all, she all but slammed into Charlotte's back.

It seemed large trucks weren't the only thing crashing into Charlotte's personal space today.

Faith shook herself out of whatever stupor she was in and saw the demolished sidewalk.

"Fun," Faith breathed sarcastically. She tilted her head, kicked some of the broken glass, and stormed into the shop.

The truck driver watched the short scene unfold and raised his eyebrow at Faith's back.

Charlotte relaxed her shoulders. "We're going through some business issues right now." Miserably, she added, "we certainly didn't need the entire entrance to our shop busted up into a million pieces."

The driver fumbled through his wallet and frowned. "I'm so sorry, it looks like I've misplaced my insurance card."

Charlotte felt herself fume and she opened her mouth as though poised to scream.

"-but here's my license," he said quickly. "I'm new to the company but they're fully insured, and although I'm sure I'll get a haranguing from my boss, it'll be taken care of quickly enough. This isn't my first accident, and it probably won't be my last."

He chuckled nervously at himself.

Charlotte tightened her lips. She pulled out her phone and snapped photos of the guy's license, wondering how many more accidents it would take before he was out on his ass.

"Is that your boss," she nodded up toward the truck cabin, hoping to catch a glimpse of the sexy man she'd seen before.

The driver threw his head back and chortled, "He wishes! Say," he changed the topic as he caught a view of the store sign above Charlotte, "what kind of business is *Faye's Fortunes*, anyway?"

"Fortune-telling and alternative health," muttered Charlotte as she returned her attention to the back of his license and lined up her phone for a photo.

"You're a psychic?"

He bore the same mischievous and ridiculing grin that cynical old men tended to have around herself, Faith, and their little divination shop in Fallstaff, Missouri.

"Actually, no," She looked at the name and address on the driver's license, and mocked "Mr. Jefferson from St. Louis-"

"-Mark, please."

"-My partner is the psychic," she waved over her shoulder to where Faith had charged past them, "I'm a massage therapist, and I practice Reiki." *Although not much anymore, these days.*

Mark smiled, and Charlotte prepared herself to school him on Reiki and the benefits of holistic health.

"Darius used to do that, and he could certainly use it; he hurt his arm moving a crate of beer yesterday," Mark shrugged his shoulder toward the handsome man in the truck. He took his license back from her stunned palm and shoved it into his front pocket. Then he checked his wristwatch. "Shoot, I have to get him back to the bar-"

Now it was Charlotte's turn to raise an eyebrow.

Mark's face brightened, "You should stop by his bar next time you're in the city. Jefferson's?"

"Jefferson's bar in St. Louis," Charlotte rolled her eyes, "Should have opened it in Jefferson City so nobody can forget it."

"We tried, but had to build where the customers were," Mark said thoughtfully. He seemed to shake himself out of his daydreaming and took his license back from Charlotte.

She softened. "I don't find myself in the big city often, but maybe I'll stop by and get that drink from you someday."

"It's Darius's bar now. I used to be the chef there, but-" Mark stopped himself from talking, then straightened, "-but your drinks are on me. He'll understand."

Charlotte looked up toward the truck, but Darius was still out of view. "Do you two often drive over sidewalks together?"

He shuffled his feet in the broken glass and shrugged. "Can't teach an old chef new trick, I guess."

## CHAPTER TWO

"Well, that guy is certain his insurance will cover it, but it's a real mess out there," Charlotte called out to Faith as she approached the back office. She surveyed the shop's lobby and realized the inside of their store was a real mess, as well. She made a mental note to unpack more of their merchandise and tidy the place up a bit later that day.

Perhaps they needed to add more space or change their displays to attract more customers.

When she entered the office, she saw Faith trying and failing to insert feathers into her hair.

Charlotte grumbled and shook her head.

"Nuh-uh," she waved Faith's hands away and took over inserting the feathers delicately. It wouldn't take long to transform her friend from simple, klutzy Faith into majestic psychic Faye, but Faith clearly couldn't do it herself.

Faith cheered, "What am I ever going to do without you?"

Charlotte dropped her jaw, affronted. "Why would you say something like that? Am I dying? You'd better not be ending our partnership. I just spent the last half hour screaming at a truck driver for ruining our entryway, so I'm doing my part."

"No, silly goose, I would never break up with you! But if we keep losing money like this, there isn't going to be a shop for us to be partners in."

"Then you'll be the one out on your butt," Charlotte tore out a few bent feathers and reinserted them, "I'm the one making the most money here."

Faith frowned. "Maybe instead of a fortune shop offering massages, we should change it to a massage parlor offering tarot readings."

"Nah," Charlotte scoffed, quickly finishing the feathers and moving on to applying Faye's eyeshadow. "Creeps would mistake a massage place for a sex shop or something. I like my current clientele; I just need more of them. They'll come."

To herself she added, *I hope.*

"I admire your positivity," Faith said.

Charlotte hid her self-doubt.

Within a few minutes, Charlotte's cosmetic skills had fully transformed her friend into an illustrious and mystical fortune teller.

Faith threw on a robe and twirled herself around the room. "Speaking of pavement," she crooned, "let me see what kind of damage was done out there."

"Dressed like that?" Charlotte eyed her with skepticism. Faith certainly looked the part of an ominous soothsayer but didn't quite fit in on the streets of a small Midwest town.

Faith lowered her voice and resounded, "I am the all-knowing oracle of a divination shop, and I declare that walking outside to survey my lands shall invoke the great spirit to send customers my way."

Charlotte scoffed at her friend's silliness. "Alright then, magic lady. You go outside and use your psychic powers to create some customers. I'm going to prep my massage table. Maybe if I sprinkle it with extra love, I can invoke the spirits to send me some customers, too."

"Watch it with the love sprinkling," Faye teased her, "we run a clean business here."

Faye danced herself out of the office and Charlotte heard the shop bells chime as her friend opened the door.

She heard Faith say to a customer, "I know everything. Please, do come in again my child."

Charlotte couldn't help herself from rolling her eyes as she ducked into her massage studio. She looked around at the older bedsheets that were starting to pill, a few stray lotions that hadn't seen use in days, and her dusty shelves lined with energy crystals that didn't appear to have any energy left in them.

She hoped her psychic friend could pull off a bigger income today, because Charlotte had no regular clients scheduled. Besides a few customers she'd had earlier in the week, their business was barely fledgling on a *good* day.

She looked down at her hands, which felt lifeless and empty, as though her healing gift had long faded away with their chances at financial success.

With a completely busted sidewalk and no new, steady customers, she feared their shop wouldn't survive the month.

# CHAPTER THREE

Her massage room was completely clean, but she straightened the pillows again anyway, just for something to do. As she bent under the table to tighten a leg that didn't need to be tightened, her phone buzzed.

She looked at the phone and saw her friend Sloane's name.

Charlotte sighed. At her best, Sloane was a lonely, jobless accountant who just needed someone to talk to. At her worst, she was suffering a full-blown panic attack over something that would, for anyone else, be completely innocuous.

Charlotte hoped for lonely.

"Hey babe," Charlotte angled her way out from under the massage table but stayed on the floor. She spoke in a whisper so as not to disturb Faith in the other room.

"Charlie? Are you at work?" Sloane's voice was panicked and hurried. She also spoke in a whisper, which Charlotte found odd since Sloane lived alone.

"Yeah, it's daytime. You should be working too, technically."

"I have no time for that. Someone new just moved in up the road, and he's staring at me."

Charlotte put her elbow on her knee and rubbed her forehead. "He's probably staring at you because you're staring at him."

"Oh," Sloane's tone changed. "Right. I'll try stepping back from the window and then checking again. Can you maybe come by tonight and find out who he is?"

After a long, financially stressful day, visiting Sloane out past Jefferson City would be a chore, but Charlotte sighed, "Yeah. I'm not expecting many customers today, so I'll leave a bit early and swing by your house, okay? If the new person is still there, I'll introduce myself."

"Are you sure? It's a little out of your way."

Charlotte nodded and rolled her eyes back in her head. She was glad Sloane couldn't see her. "Yeah, I got you. Somebody in St. Louis owes me a drink, anyway."

"Oooo," Sloane gushed, "did wound-up Charlie finally find a date?"

"No!" Charlotte insisted but felt her heart thud slightly at the memory of the stunning specimen she'd barely glimpsed earlier in the day. She collected herself and continued, "I do not have the patience nor time for *any* man, especially one that lives over two hours out of my way. You know this."

She overheard commotion in her shop's reception room and peered through the crack in the door. To Sloane, she said quickly, "but I do have time for you. I'll see you later."

Sloane thanked her profusely and Charlotte hung up. While it was a chore to manage one friend's business and another friend's paranoia, Charlotte would welcome Sloane's accountant-savvy ear to bounce their financial problems around in.

Her business partner Faith was far too close to their money troubles.

Through the crack in her massage room door, Charlotte watched Faith's customer angrily charging at a man in the doorway, and Faith frantically trying to hold the woman back.

She stepped back from the doorway and listened to the interaction. The last thing their business needed was a couple fighting about what they'd learned in a psychic reading, but at the same time she knew Faith was probably devastated by what was happening.

Faith hated to predict things wrong or destroy lives.

Even though Charlotte didn't fully understand fortune-telling, she had to back up her friend in every situation.

She heard the door slam shut, and Faith groaned.

Charlotte stepped carefully out of the room, noted the couple had left, and ran to Faith's side to comfort her, "it was bound to happen," she laughed, only guessing at what had transpired. "You probably aren't the first Psychic to ruin a relationship, and you won't be the last."

The dark panic in Faith's face lightened, and she smiled as she fell into Charlotte's arms. "I'm a mess and this business is a mess," Faith said.

"Well, you're on your own with *your* mess," Charlotte assured her, "but I'm with you on the business side. We'll make it work."

Charlotte smiled, maintaining her part in their relationship as the upbeat, forward-thinking bestie, but she couldn't help thinking to herself *But I have no idea how to make it work.*

## CHAPTER FOUR

After a day of yelling at truck drivers and cleaning a room that didn't need to be cleaned, for customers that never came, Charlotte was looking forward to a break. But the long drive and visit to her childhood friend's house wasn't the relaxing experience her body desired. Sloane was stressed about grocery delivery, mail, and her nagging paranoia about all her new neighbors.

"I'm on my way to visit this bar in St. Louis," offered Charlotte, sitting at Sloane's kitchen island and looking at the empty shelves. Knowing it would be fruitless, she asked, "Why don't you try coming with me?"

"You know I can't come with you," Sloane uttered, and Charlotte wondered if her friend was finally admitting she had a problem leaving her own house.

The moment disappeared when Sloane continued, "I still have too much unpacking to do."

"Sloane, you need a therapist," Charlotte stood up to leave. She'd been there nearly three hours and Sloane didn't have any wine, so it had been three hours of

Sloane's self-deceit, spying on her boring neighbors, zero business advice, and no booze to soften any of the blow.

"I don't have a problem," insisted Sloane as they descended the staircase toward her front door, "I just like the indoors more than the outdoors. That's a normal thing. Lots of people are homebodies."

*But none of them will literally faint if they have to walk outside their apartment*, thought Charlotte.

"Okay," Charlotte relented. Fighting Sloane on her psychological problems was a waste of time. "Have you found any new clients lately?"

"I still have a few contracts from before the move," Sloane bit her lip, "but it's hard to find new people when-"

"When you never get out?"

"I was going to say, Charles," Sloane scoffed, using a silly childhood nickname Charlotte had never liked, "-when you're still trying to move in."

*It's been almost a month*, Charlotte wanted to retort. Instead, she resisted. "If we had any money, you know we'd hire you to help with Faye's Fortunes."

"I know, babe. I can't wait to see your store one day," Sloane lied as she opened the front door for Charlotte. She hid behind it as though the outside world might leap right in and attack.

Charlotte stepped outside and felt the door half close behind her. She looked back to see Sloane peering through the crack with one eyeball.

"I've got to get some sleep, Slo. Busy day tomorrow with all the zero customers I expect," Charlotte laughed at herself, "I'll see if any of them have any business for you."

"You're the best, Charlie! Love you," Sloane gushed as she slammed the door in Charlotte's face.

*Weird way to show love, but okay,* Charlotte shrugged at the closed door.

Despite the distance and late hour, she continued East toward St. Louis, checking her pockets for tip money for the bartender. She desperately needed that truck driver's free drink to wash away her stress. She wished she had the cash for more than the free one. Maybe then she'd be able to sleep without worrying about her business.

#

If Charlotte thought Fallstaff, Faye's Fortunes, and Sloane's new townhouse were in the middle of nowhere, this bar was in the absolute sticks in comparison. Although technically within the greater St. Louis limits, it was in a dark, industrial area, and on a weekend night the streets were vacant. There wasn't anyone around anywhere, nor any lights from the bar to show her where it was. She drove around the address three times before she figured out where she was supposed to go.

The entrance to the bar faced the back alley of a parking lot rather than the street, so it was nearly impossible to see on the second loop around the block, let alone the first. It was only on the third try, when she was about to give up, that Charlotte finally found it. She'd pulled her Honda Accord over so she could try to get a GPS streetview image on her phone, and that's when she'd spotted a thin beam of light in an alley.

There wasn't anyone around, and there was no sign above the building, but when she turned off her engine she heard some faint, piped music.

She got out of her car and walked toward the light, which broke through a window almost completely covered with beer advertisements. It was not welcoming at all.

The bar door creaked as she opened it, and a bell rang to welcome her, reminding her of the little bells that rang at *Faye's Fortunes*. At the sound, she instantly felt welcome rather than creeped out, but she knew a back alley in an industrial park at night still wasn't the safest place to be alone.

The pub itself was empty save for one vagrant talking into his whiskey glass. There didn't appear to be any service staff at all.

The man looked up and slurred in her direction, "Heyy-oh, 'tis a lady!"

It could have been a frightening experience, but his strange acknowledgement of her was so funny, Charlotte couldn't help but chuckle. She searched the deepest parts of her gut instinct to try and find her caution detector, but nothing came up. Deeming him safe and friendly, she sat down with a seat between them. Far enough to be safe, but close enough to chat if he had the wherewithal to do so.

She could use a conversation that wasn't Faye's drama, Sloane's paranoia, or her business on the brink of collapse. "How's it going," she asked the man.

He leaned back in surprise, as though he'd thought she was an apparition before. Realizing she was real and speaking to him, he straightened his chest like a prideful animal boasting about a win. She'd seen this manly display play out a thousand times in her life, but from this disheveled old tramp it only made her giggle even more.

"Darius here was just getting me another drink," the man said, waving his empty glass at nothing.

Charlotte's heart fluttered, remembering the truck driver's handsome son that she'd only caught a quick glance at earlier that day.

He wasn't there, though. She was pretty sure of that. She leaned forward and took a second look behind the bar, just to make sure she wasn't losing her mind.

"There's no one here but us," she said to the man.

"Oh, I don't know," the man slurred and stared into his empty glass like it had asked him a question.

"That would be me," a voice came from behind them. Charlotte turned to see the dark, muscled pair of arms she'd seen in the truck earlier, struggling to hold two large boxes of whiskey bottles. One of the strong arms was still in the sling. Behind the cases of whiskey, she assumed his smoldering set of eyes lit up the entire room.

Charlotte blew air out from her lips, then turned it into a laugh and shook herself out of her trance. Not knowing quite how to stop the sudden rush of blood to her face, she darted over to help with one of the crates.

Darius paused while she grabbed one, and with a small, sexy groan he seemed to melt with the ease of stress off his hurt arm. She took a quick glance at his biceps to try and figure out what part of it was injured, but his muscles all looked damn fine and in beautiful working order.

If she'd lost her magic eye for sore spots, this man's perfect muscles weren't making it easy to bring them back.

When the crate was removed from in front of his face, immediately his brooding eyes sucked her into their magic, and she realized she was staring at them a bit too long. She felt her cheeks flush, looked down at the whiskey, and wondered if he too was staring at her just a moment too long as well.

She didn't dare look back at him lest she be so flustered she dropped the heavy crate in her arms, so she turned toward the bar instead.

"This is a lot of whiskey, I hope it's not all for your friend over there," she nodded toward the man at the bar.

"Nah, he's done drinking. Isn't that right Perry?"

"I don't think so, man." Perry waved his glass in the air and tapped it with his finger.

Darius moved past Charlotte quickly, as though running away from her. He rounded the bar and said to Perry, "I have to shut down old man, there's no one here tonight."

"But my girlfriend just arrived!" Perry waved at Charlotte, who stayed busy by placing her crate on top of the bar.

Darius put his crate down beside Charlotte's and gave her a side-eye look.

Charlotte laughed and shook her head in the negative, just in case her relationship status with the bum wasn't obvious.

Now it was Darius's turn to chuckle and shake his head. "You wish, Perry."

"If you're not open, I'll come back another time," Charlotte said, removing some of the whiskey bottles from the crate automatically, as though she were at her own divination shop lining up crystal balls on a display case.

She placed thee bottles next to each other and watched the lights bounce between them. She may not be able to read a crystal ball very well, but she could certainly see herself in this whiskey.

Darius took her bottles and placed them in a cabinet under the bar, pulling her out of her thoughtful visions. He whispered, "I can stay open a little longer-"

Perry waved his glass at Darius.

"-but not for you, Perry. You've had more than enough, and you owe me forty dollars just for tonight."

Perry growled, "did your old man let you raise the price, son? We had an agreement!"

"Forty is even less than Dad used to charge *you*, old man. I don't think you realize how much you've had to drink."

Perry looked at his arm as though a watch were there, and his mouth formed an O.

Charlotte laughed. It was so refreshing to just be amused instead of stressed.

"Well then, I'll be on my way," Perry stumbled off his stool.

Charlotte bolted toward him and caught him before he fell.

"Are you my new nurse? These drugs aren't working," Perry slurred.

Charlotte walked him out the exit.

"Will he be okay," she asked as the door closed behind him.

"He'll be fine, I'm pretty sure he's currently living by the dumpster behind the funeral home right now. It's only a block away."

Charlotte relaxed. Then she remembered she was alone in a strange bar, and the only other patron had just left. "I'll come back another night," she said, pushing the door back open.

"No, stay. Please." Darius rushed to remove the bottles from the counter and wipe it down. "I only told him I was closing so he'd get some sleep."

Darius looked around the room at the empty seats, dart boards, billiard tables, and barstools that sat clean and unused all day, "-and also because I have no customers."

Charlotte smiled and saddled up to the bar again. "Well that's perfect," she smiled, "because I like drinking alone, and I have money burning a hole in my pocket."

That last part was a lie since her massage business had completely dried up, but Darius didn't need to know that.

# CHAPTER FIVE

Charlotte watched Darius unload the whiskey bottles into the cabinet and found herself with nothing to say. She wondered if her tongue was tied, or if she was just exhausted from the long day of the poor business, the meeting with her mentally unwell friend, and the even longer drive to St. Louis.

Or was the strong, handsome bartender in front of her sending shock waves through her system?

She needed a drink. "You're Darius, right? Mark's son?"

Darius kept one whiskey bottle out from underneath the cabinet, and instead placed it on a mirrored shelf above the bar. Then he turned and smiled, "That depends, are you here for sidewalk money?"

His cut jaw and sexy smile sent shivers through Charlotte, but she held her own. "I'm hoping the trucking company's insurance covers that, but I am owed a favor."

His smile turned to a confused frown. If he could possibly be sexier while concerned and worried, he was.

Charlotte melted.

She quickly added, "I don't know if your Dad mentioned this to you earlier, but-"

Darius's shoulders fell even further, and he winced in a bit of pain. "Let me guess, he offered you free drinks?"

Charlotte smiled meekly and shrugged. She noted the pain was in the top of his left shoulder, and she longed to reach over and pull it out of him. *If I still have any Reiki healing skills left in me,* she thought.

Darius's smile returned after a split second. He puffed out his chest as if to steady himself and laughed, "That sounds about right for my Dad - making *me* poor to save face with the ladies. What would you like?"

"This whiskey looks interesting, I'll try it."

"Terrible choice," Darius took two glasses down from the shelf, "this is the cheap shit I serve guys who never pay me, like Perry." He nodded toward the door and Charlotte caught herself staring at his fine, stubbled jaw.

She shook herself and sat back down at the bar. "Well, I don't want you to waste the good stuff on me. All whiskeys seem to burn on the way down anyway," Charlotte pointed out the two glasses he held in his devastatingly rugged hands, "Just the one is fine too, thanks."

"The second one is for me. I'll probably close up after this."

"On a Saturday?"

Darius brought a different bottle down from a high shelf again and popped the cork. He sniffed it and seemed pleased. He offered it to Charlotte to smell.

She shook her head. She wouldn't know what she was smelling, anyway.

"This is an industrial area. Nobody shows up on Saturdays." He poured out two shots and added wistfully, "nobody really shows up at any time at all anymore."

"I know that life. Business is terrible for me, too."

"What's your business?" Darius handed a shot to her.

Charlotte admired the pour before tasting it. The smoky heat melted her throat and relaxed her entire body. It felt like a massage for the insides.

"Massage," she remembered he'd asked a question and she shook herself out of her pleasure. She would need to stop after one glass if she expected to get home later.

"I studied massage years ago," Darius said.

"Your Dad mentioned it in passing, but I was kind of busy swearing at him," Charlotte chuckled nervously. She hoped he wouldn't get upset that she'd sworn at his father.

Darius laughed, easing her worries. He downed the shot in one gulp and started rinsing out his glass.

Charlotte asked, "just the one?"

Darius dried the glass and set it back on the shelf, "I actually don't drink. It's bad for business."

"I wonder if that's what I'm doing wrong, too?" Charlotte laughed and downed her drink as well. It melted like a candle in her chest, and she realized in that instance the difference between good whiskey and bad whiskey. She promised herself that from then on it would be top shelf or nothing at all.

She stood from the bar and turned toward the door.

"Don't leave," Darius begged, "I have even better whiskey I promise."

"I'm not leaving, silly," Charlotte rounded the bar toward the other side, and brought her glass toward the sink, "I'm going to rinse this out and then get some customers in here for you."

"I think Perry is long gone by now," laughed Darius. He took the glass from her and waved her away from the sink.

Charlotte walked toward the front window and started tearing down the ads that were covering them up. While she did so, she unbuttoned the top of her blouse and squeezed her breasts together. While she was tall enough to reach all the papers on the window, she still grabbed a chair and stood on it, so she was forced to bend and show off her cleavage through the glass.

"What in the good lord's name are you doing with your body?" asked Darius, approaching from behind to help her remove papers.

"I know what sells," Charlotte laughed, "and it's definitely not beer ads covering all these windows."

"Please don't subject yourself to this."

"To what? Redecorating?"

After tearing down the higher ads, she turned to step down off the chair. Darius held out a hand for her. She tried to maintain her playful persona, but when she grabbed his strong hand, she suddenly felt weightless, and she tripped over her own heels. He caught her as she stumbled off the chair and held her tight for a split second. His shoulder buckled, and he winced but recovered quickly.

Flustered, she looked down at her chest as she collected herself. Her right breast has almost popped completely out of her unbuttoned blouse. As Darius sucked in a gasp and let her go, she laughed and readjusted her shirt. "I like to redecorate with my boobs partway out, what?"

Darius caught his tongue in his throat and forced himself to chuckle. He stepped back and looked elsewhere. She could tell he was doing his best to respect her space.

He looked at anything but her as he asked, "Do you think uncovering the windows will help?"

"Of course. Why were they covered anyway?"

"When we had to shut down temporarily, it was to keep burglars out. Then we rushed so fast to reopen I just neglected to clean this place up. My Dad couldn't afford to work here as a chef anymore because we weren't serving food, so-"

"-so you didn't need to advertise it as a restaurant anymore, just an industrial bar," Charlotte nodded. "I get it. Times changed-"

"-and the people disappeared," sighed Darius.

A moment of gentle understanding washed between them.

Darius asked, "okay, the windows aren't covered. Now what?"

"Now we have to draw attention into this back parking lot." Charlotte playfully shook her chest, "I could flash my boobs on the street corner-"

"-No!" Darius held up his hand to block her chest from his view, "I don't even know you but that's where I draw the line!"

Charlotte could tell she'd made him blush. The shy way he tried to look anywhere but her was a dead giveaway.

"I have an old neon light in the back," Darius said. "I could see if it works. It doesn't say the bar name, but-"

"It doesn't have to. If we can hang it on the side of the building that faces the street, it'll let people know there is life here," Charlotte insisted.

Just then, the door of the bar opened behind them, and a surly man wearing a reflective jacket came in. He ogled Charlotte a few seconds too long, then asked Darius "you open? I just need a bathroom."

"Yeah," Darius moved in front of Charlotte as though protecting her from the man's possessing gaze, but at the same time he smiled kindly and waved toward the back of the bar. "Come right in."

When the man had found the restroom, Darius turned to Charlotte and waved at her without looking. "Damn, you're good. Now please button that up."

"Spoilsport," Charlotte laughed at his pathetic display, but re-did the button across her cleavage. "If you don't like these epic boobs lighting up your entryway, then you're gonna have to go find that neon light."

# CHAPTER SIX

After using the restroom, the stranger bought himself a quick shot of rum. On his way out he said he'd swing by the next time he was in town.

Darius found the neon light in the back and showed it to Charlotte. "I'll get Dad to help me hang it," he said, and started tucking the light on the floor behind the bar.

Charlotte held out her hand for it "I'll do it, just show me where to go. What did you do to your left shoulder?"

"You noticed that, huh? The doc said it's repetitive strain. I'm the only one here hauling booze crates at night, and I help my Dad with deliveries during the day. It was bound to kill me sometime."

Darius seemed to wince while mentioning the work he did, and Charlotte watched his otherwise strong body weaken with the pressure of trying to run a small business all by himself. She longed to reach out and rub out his shoulder pain, his stress, and maybe some of her own sexual tension out of both of them.

Darius asked, "You sure you can handle it?"

"What?" Charlotte dropped her jaw. Had he read her mind?

"The sign? Are you sure you can handle hanging it outside?"

"Oh," she shook her head, completely flustered. "Yes, of course. I unpack decorative shiny things at my shop all day. This is just another type of whimsical rock to put on display."

Darius laughed. Together, they went outside.

Charlotte climbed up onto a fire escape, took the light Darius held up for her, and walked across the roof to the front of the building facing the street. She found a hook and an outlet to attach it to, and she plugged it in. It advertised a beer brand in pinks and greens.

She called, "Can you see it from the street?"

Darius moved out of the alley and stood back from the building. "Yes, but I don't know if it'll stand the weather," he noted.

"It just needs to stay here long enough to get some customers in the door, then you can invest in a better one." Charlotte paused to both admire her work and look out over the industrial area. She could see downtown St. Louis from way up there, but not much else.

However, within a few moments of turning the light on, a large U-Haul pulled into the parking lot. A man and a woman climbed out.

"You're brilliant! Come on," Darius waved at Charlotte to come back down.

As he came around to meet her below the fire escape, she chuckled down, "I wish I could magically attract clients to *my* store like this."

"Turns out all you need is a neon sign."

"I still think it was my cleavage," Charlotte heaved herself down the last part of the fire escape and slipped over her heel.

Darius caught her waist and sucked in a breath of air as she landed softly on him.

"I'm sorry," she put her hand on his shoulder and moved away from his arm lest she hurt it anymore.

"It's fine," he lied, gently stabilizing her before letting her go.

She felt the muscular warmth of his body through her thin shirt. His arms briefly encircled her shoulders, and she almost went limp in them. Her nerves tingled and her body filled with a thousand extra doses of dopamine and estrogen.

He pulled back and stretched out his arms, almost pushing her away as he steadied her. He coughed, "all good?"

She'd briefly forgotten where she was, standing in a cold alleyway under a dirty fire escape, with a devastatingly sexy bartender. She shivered as though feigning a chill, when in actuality she was trying desperately to get over her sudden flush of desire.

"All good," she lied.

"Great! Let's go - we've got customers!" Darius spun around and bolted toward the bar, as though the last ten seconds hadn't even happened.

Charlotte watched him go. Before she took a step, she whispered, "*we?*"

# CHAPTER SEVEN

As if by magic, Jefferson's pub came alive, and more cargo trucks and pickups spotted the sign and pulled into the parking lot. Charlotte helped behind the bar, which gave Darius's arm a reprieve and offered him a chance to chat up the new customers. The girls fawned over him. The guys did, too. He was charming and sexy and handsome, and Charlotte herself could barely keep her eyes off him while she poured drinks. She thanked her lucky stars that most of the customers wanted draught beer and not something that required measuring and thinking. It had been too many years since she'd worked behind a bar.

When the final customers started drifting out around 2am, Darius collected glasses from the tables.

"That was a great night," he said. "The first one in a while."

Charlotte wiped down the bar. "That's awesome, I'm glad I was here for it."

"You were the *cause* of it," Darius insisted.

"I don't think opening the windows really made that much of a difference-"

"No, you're right." He walked over to where she stood and leaned in, "The difference was you."

Charlotte felt his body enter her energy field and her entire body felt warm, like the vibration of a thousand African animals storming across the Serengeti. She all but shut her eyes and leaned in for a kiss.

He leaned past her and opened the dishwasher, pulling out the wire drawer like he hadn't just filled her entire body with electrical jolts intended to raise her long-dead sex life from the grave.

"I should go," Charlotte stammered, "I've gotta work early." She fiddled with the cloth in her hands and then threw it onto the bar, racing to adjust herself back to her senses.

Darius remained bent over the dishwasher, and she admired his fine tight ass as she wondered how to finagle her way around it and out of the bar area.

Just as she was awkwardly about to move past him, he stood back up and drew close to her again, "wait," he whispered to her.

She felt her body start to melt again. Before she could collapse into a puddle of imagined fantasy, he moved away again and opened the till.

He pulled out a stack of bills and handed it to her.

Shaking herself out of her ecstasy yet again, she coughed "oh no, it's fine. I sipped your good whiskey all evening."

"Please, take it," said Darius, forcing it into her hands. "You brought life to this bar and the customers loved you."

Charlotte almost pushed the money back at him again, but a niggling voice from the deep recesses of her mind reminded her that her own business was only a few weeks away from complete collapse. Any money she could get to help with bills could keep Faith and herself afloat until work improved.

She had to put her shop first.

She nodded, took the stack of bills, and moved her hand toward her chest.

Darius watched as she slid the bills under the top of her bra strap, his mouth slightly open.

*Good*, she thought, *at least I'm not the only one with a runaway mind.*

She angled past him before she could let her body betray her any further, and she all but ran to the door.

"Please come back again," Darius begged, "tomorrow night. I need you."

"I have work, I'm sorry," Charlotte fumbled over the doorknob. She felt her nipples harden with the rush of chilly night air, and if it were possible to disappear immediately, she begged for it as she launched herself out into the breeze.

"Can I walk you to your car?" Darius called after her.

"No, it's right here," she bolted across the parking lot, waving awkwardly toward her beat-up corolla, trying to prevent him from seeing the flush of sex that had overtaken her physical form.

He watched her from the corner, surveying the parking lot like an army guard.

She took another look at his fierce form as she started her car, and her entire body filled with desperation.

He waved at her as she drove past, and she tried not to look. She wondered if he could sense the dampness in her panties, too.

Before getting on the freeway, she pulled over, took a deep breath, and wiped the sweat from her chest. As she did so, the stack of bills tumbled out of her bra. Now that she had a moment to really look at them, she did a quick calculation and it looked like a week's worth of Reiki massages in one night of bartending.

"Daaaaamn," she said slowly.

If she could just figure out how to work *and* play, she might do another night of this.

## CHAPTER EIGHT

Sunday morning, sunlight beat down through the bedroom curtain like a tyrannical nation was launching an epic war against Charlotte's face. She groaned and rubbed her head. The previous evening she'd had more than the one whiskey shot she'd intended, and the long drive hadn't gotten her home until nearly five o'clock.

The memory of pouring shots, laughing with customers, and occasionally tripping into Darius's strong arms came flooding back. Charlotte felt like she'd been pleasured a million times over, even though nothing sexual had happened at all.

She rinsed her face in her small bathroom, and as the rush of cool water woke her up, she relived the endorphin high she'd felt the night before. It had been such a long time since she'd felt any electricity flow through her body like that.

She wished she had those same vibes in her real job. Desperate to clear the fog in her skull, she stopped at the small coffee shop below her apartment, and ordered a quadruple shot for herself and a latte for Faith.

She'd downed the espresso by the time she got to Faye's Fortunes.

The sidewalk in front of the shop was still torn to shreds, but Faith had swept a path to the front door the previous evening. At least the shop still appeared open - not that they had many customers who might otherwise be confused.

Charlotte let herself in and locked the shop door behind her. Although they didn't technically open for another hour, she turned on the Open sign. She also opened the dark curtains a little to let the morning light in. Faith never liked doing that, as it 'ruined the mysterious aesthetic,' but Charlotte loved the way the morning sun made their crystals and artifacts shimmer. It brought life to the place, and she hoped it might bring some sales energy, as well.

As she adjusted a display of Tarot decks, a knock sounded at the door. She looked at the clock. It was still at least forty-five minutes until their official opening time, but she wasn't about to turn down business when they needed it.

She unlocked the door and opened it to a handsome man in an expensive, tailored suit. Charlotte was taken aback. The suit was very un-Fallstaff and un-weekend morning, and definitely not the fortune telling and Reiki vibe.

Charlotte feared it was their landlord coming to hit them up for the store's rent, but that wasn't due for another week.

She asked, "Can I help you?"

"Halton, Pete Halton," he didn't reach out a hand to shake, but paused as if waiting for her to recognize the name. When she didn't speak, he said "I'm interested in buying the space across the street," he tilted his large shoulder slightly as though that would make the view clearer behind his broad shoulders. It didn't.

Charlotte bent to look around him and noted an old tire shop that had gone out of business long before her shop had opened. She and Faith had welcomed the abandoned lot, as it created extra parking spaces in Fallstaff's tiny downtown core - not that anyone ever used it for Faye's Fortunes.

Charlotte smiled, "I'm afraid I don't know the owner, that building has been closed for quite a while."

"I figured," the man looked over her shoulder and peered inside the shop behind her. She started to feel exposed and nervous. He continued, "I just wanted to let you know that we might be making some changes in a couple of weeks."

"Oh?" A shudder crept through her blood, but she fended it off. "We love our changing town. What type of business do you run?"

"It's a market, of sorts," he said vaguely.

"That's great," Charlotte faked interest, "What a lovely addition."

"Yeah, we'll see," he looked up at their *Faye's Fortunes* sign. "I actually just wanted to check if you guys were still in business."

Charlotte kept the door half closed on him, but waved her hand around their shop and kept the smile plastered on her face. "Yup, still here and going strong," she lied.

"We'll see," he said again, and kicked a few glass sidewalk stones. "If this plaza were gone, Fallstaff would get more visibility from the highway."

"The nail salon and our shop do just fine," Charlotte lied.

"Maybe you can join my new development," he nodded over his shoulder. Then, he backed away from the door, looked down the plaza at the empty stores that lay between Faye's Fortunes and the nail salon, and shrugged knowingly at Charlotte.

He turned and crossed the street without looking both directions.

Charlotte watched him walk away and slowly closed the door. She shut off the Open sign.

"That was so weird," she said aloud. A crystal ball hanging in the window seemed to tremble, as though it were agreeing with her.

# CHAPTER NINE

Although Sunday was typically one of their busiest days, business was still slow. Faith had a couple of kids wanting tarot readings, but she didn't charge them much, and Charlotte had one two-hour standard massage, which made her fingers feel a little numb by the time she was done.

The client offered two hundred and fifty dollars for the abnormally long physical massage, however, which Charlotte graciously accepted. It might just cover their business phone bill for the month.

Although her partner didn't say it, she could tell Faith was relieved by the money as well. At five o'clock, when it was clear business would be dry for the dinner hour, Faith offered to rub Charlotte's hands.

"You're a godsend," Charlotte said to her, as they faced each other over her massage table. Faith started gently caressing the backs of her hands.

Faith gushed, "no, *you* are, Charlie. You're the one bringing in the most money here." She turned

Charlotte's palms over to rub the inside. As she did, she drew her finger along the lines in Charlotte's palms.

"Hmm," Faith mumbled, and continued to massage Charlie's hand while staring into it.

"What? Don't tell me the entire trajectory of my life has changed," Charlotte laughed and fluttered her hands, but she raised an eyebrow in curiosity.

"Oh, it's nothing, I just noticed some new lines developing. I guess I haven't read your palms in a bit."

"Are you saying I'm getting wrinkly?! I've been lied to by my ancestors!" Charlotte frowned at her hands.

Faith laughed, "they're not wrinkles! Maybe you've just been working too hard and your hands are showing it. That's a good thing," she slumped her shoulders a little, "you're the one carrying our business, that's for sure. These hands are magic."

"They'd better stay that way, I'm not ready to age yet," Charlotte joked, but was still a little worried that her healing hands might give up on her before they really got their business going again.

Seriously, she asked Faith, "what do you see?"

"Well," Faith looked closer at Charlotte's palms, opening and closing them, and sensing their energy as the fine lines seemed to darken and lighten at different pressure points. "You're cheating on someone. You have multiple loves."

Charlotte scoffed, "I think you're getting me confused with that weird couple you broke up the other day." She referred to the previous day's drama with Faith's client.

"No," Faith said a little too quickly, "There's something here. Maybe it's not romantic, but your heart is in two places. What is that about?"

It was the bar, Charlotte knew. It's not as though she'd fallen in love with Darius in one night, but his touch reminded her of something she'd buried long ago. Not to mention she'd had a ton of fun working the bar and chatting up guests all evening, and it had brought out her joyful, social side. It was an extroversion that was lacking at the Fortune telling business, since they got so few customers during the days anymore.

"It's nothing," Charlotte insisted after a long moment.

Faith raised an eyebrow. Charlotte knew her partner didn't believe a word she was saying.

"Okay Charlie," Faith patted her palms and teased, "maybe it *is* wrinkles then."

Charlotte gasped, "bitch" and she swatted Faith's hands.

The two of them fell into a fit of giggles, then Faith took Charlotte's hands back and began massaging them again.

"What are you up to tonight," Faith asked, rubbing Charlotte's index finger. She peered a little too closely at the lines that dotted it. "Do you want to come over and watch TV? I'm probably going to be evicted this week, we might as well get some use out of the cable I'm stealing from my neighbor."

Charlotte laughed, "I'd love to, babe, but I'm kinda worn out."

Faith looked from Charlotte's hands into her face, but Charlotte kept her sights squarely on her own palms. She knew her psychic friend could see right through her lies, but she also knew she'd drop it.

Truthfully, Charlotte wanted to drive back to Jefferson's bar and watch Darius entertain his guests again. It was much more entertaining for her senses than anything on TV.

"That makes sense," Faith said with intense skepticism, drawing Charlotte completely out of her fantasies.

Faith picked up Charlotte's hand and held the palm up in her face, "These poor mitts of yours are exhausted. Try and rest your wrinkly hands up tonight, you old bat."

Charlotte shrieked and swatted her again.

# CHAPTER TEN

When Charlotte finally arrived at Jefferson's Pub, there were a few cars in the parking lot and one 18-wheeler that she hadn't seen the day before. She hoped this meant the place was even livelier than it had been on Saturday.

Although the front window faced the back of the parking lot, she was pleased to see it looked more welcoming without all the advertisements hanging in it. She could see several customers had bellied up to the bar.

When she entered, they cheered "Heyyy!"

"I'm glad your lady friend is back," drawled Perry, spitting on the counter. "This right here was turning into a sausage fest."

Darius smiled and wiped the counter down like nothing had happened.

"I'm glad someone missed me," laughed Charlotte.

Another man slurred "What's your name, hot stuff?"

"Watch yourself," Darius scolded him.

Rather than being irritated, Charlotte was thrilled he'd admonished the guy so that she didn't have to. A woman standing up for herself in an industrial bar probably wouldn't go over so well.

"Charlie," she said to the man.

"No, they call me Chuck," drooled the guy.

"No, that's my name. Charlie."

Chuck overreacted, "That's a man's name!"

A few of the other patrons laughed at him. "Leave her alone and go home Chuck, you're drunk," someone said.

"Am not drunk! Am Chuck!" he stumbled off his seat and nearly fell to the floor.

"Okay Chuck, I think that's enough for you," Darius removed the guy's remaining beer from the bar.

"I'm not paying for a beer I didn't get to finish," Chuck ranted as he stumbled toward the bathroom.

"You never pay your tab anyway," laughed another patron.

Darius tried to smile, but Charlotte could see a worried grimace pass over his face, too. She wondered if his business troubles were like her own, or was he worried about something else? She pulled off her jacket and stuck it in a cabinet under the bar. Crouching out of view of the patrons, she whispered with enough volume to overcome the din, "I hope I didn't cause trouble already."

Darius spoke in a louder volume to assure her, "Nah. I just hope these assholes don't scare you away."

"Hey! Who you calling agg-shole," a patron bellowed.

Charlotte grabbed an apron and stood back up to tie it around her waist.

"Watch your mumbling or Darius will pull your beer away too," she teased the drunkard.

The man grabbed his beer and held it tight, eyeing Darius with suspicion.

A few other customers laughed at the interaction.

From down the bar, someone slammed his empty beer mug on the table and shouted to Charlotte, "fetch me a tankard, wen-"

"Watch it," hissed Darius.

"-when you get a minute, please," the man faltered.

Charlotte winked at Darius and walked down the bar to grab the man's mug.

"Good save," she said to him.

"He likes you," responded the man, nodding toward Darius.

"Oh?" Charlotte took the mug and started refilling it at the tap, realizing halfway through the pour that she had no idea what the man had been drinking.

He didn't seem to notice or care, "Oh yeah, definitely. I used to call his girlfriend 'wench' all day and he never chewed me out like that."

Charlotte nodded and curled her lip, but it was only to hide how uncomfortable she was feeling. *Girlfriend? What girlfriend? When?*

It bothered her how bothered she was by the casual comment.

She put the mug down in front of the customer and he pawed at it heartily, clearly not caring what was in it.

She raised an eyebrow at him and wiped down a counter to keep herself busy, but she found herself staring at Darius's lean muscular form and wondering, *and is the girlfriend still in the picture?*

# CHAPTER ELEVEN

The first couple of hours at the bar flew by. Charlotte enjoyed staying busy and talking to all the customers. It was a refreshing change from the slow, boring days at the divination shop.

But when eleven o'clock rolled around, she started to realize how long she'd been awake and working, and how little sleep she'd gotten the night before. The odd thing about zero-business days and tons-of-business nights was that they could exhaust you equally. She was ready for bed but still over two hours from home.

Darius must have noticed. At one point he tapped her on the shoulder, and Charlotte realized she'd been staring blankly into the mirror behind a bottle of Chivas Regal.

"You're somewhere else," he said, holding his sore hand on her back for an extra moment while he pulled down a bottle of Macallan 15.

She felt the warmth of his palm through her shirt, and she lost herself through the tingles his touch sent up her neck and down her spine. If she could have melted into his grip at that moment, she would have.

He may have sensed this too, as he stroked her ever so slightly, like soft massage. It had been months, maybe years since she'd received a back massage of her own.

"Hmmm," she muttered, closing her eyes. It took her a second to remember where she was and what he'd just said to her. She popped her eyes back open. "I guess it's been a long day."

Darius took his hand off her back, and the void it left felt like opening the door to an arctic wind. He looked at the tradesmen and truckers who lined the bar. "You can go, if you want," he said to her. "I can handle the rest of these guys."

"No, you can't," Perry yelled from down the bar. "She's the only reason I'm here tonight."

"Yeah, us too!" Some truckers wailed.

"Perry, you're here because you've got nowhere else to go, old man," Darius scorned.

Charlotte laughed, which woke her up a little more.

"I don't mind," she stretched, and felt the icky grip of the male gaze behind her.

Darius seemed to sense it too and stepped between her and the customers.

She shook out her arms and said, "My shop doesn't open until after noon on Mondays, so I can sleep in."

"Right on," said a customer.

Darius frowned, which made Charlotte feel warm inside.

# CHAPTER TWELVE

Darius and Charlotte worked as a team, each taking a side of the bar and chatting with the patrons. At one point, Darius leaned over her and whispered, "We haven't had this number of guests in a long time. I think you have something to do with it."

"Could also be the fact that the worst of the pandemic is over," Charlotte whispered back.

"No," he leaned forward so he could catch her eye. "It's definitely you. Thank you."

Charlotte felt the heat rise in her face, and she lost track of the numbers she was punching into the computer screen. She smiled and shook her head nervously. "It's nothing," she squeaked out.

Darius pulled glasses out of the dishwasher and dried them with a rag "I'm going to need an accountant again. I fired the last one when we had to shut down."

"You could hire my friend Sloane," Charlotte said. "She's just moved back to the area and is looking for local clients."

"Wow, you've got a solution for everything," Darius said, almost in awe.

"I just enjoy making connections," she said.

"I love making connections with you," Darius stood within a foot of her, and she felt a yearning heat rise in her body.

From behind Darius, her phone rang under the bar, pulling them both out of the moment.

"Oh gosh," Charlotte blinked and looked around at the register, trying to figure out what she was working on before.

"No worries, keep it up," Darius nodded at the computer where she was still trying to input a simple order. "I'll get your phone for you."

He turned and took a few steps, and she suddenly felt a chill. It was like all the heat energy in her body was so desperate to lunge after him, wrestle him onto the ground, and make mad love to him right there in front of everyone, that when he moved out of her aura her flesh cried in longing.

"Charlie's phone," Darius said into the cellphone and turned back toward her.

Nearing midnight on a Sunday, Charlotte figured the only two people it could be was Faith or Sloane, either of them probably needing more from her than she wanted to give them.

"Take a message," she called and returned her attention to the register.

"She's not available right now, can I ask who is calling?"

Darius pointed his head down and put a finger in his other ear to drown out the noise from the bar. His face turned serious, but Charlotte couldn't quite hear what he was saying into the phone. She finished tallying the bill, handed it to her customer, and walked over to Darius.

"No, she's not interested in that, but thanks for the chat." Darius looked at her, but behind his deep magnetic orbs of body-melting intensity, she could sense he was growing frustrated.

She held out her hand to relieve him of her phone, but he shook his head at her.

"Yeah no, I'll tell her you called but I'm sure she's not interested, thanks." He could not have pressed the end-call button any faster.

Charlotte wasn't sure if she was more upset that he'd brushed her off to answer her calls for her, that her body was fighting her every second to grab him and molest him on the floor, or that someone had called her this late on a Sunday night. Her words came out frustrated and terse, "What the hell was that about?"

Darius raised his eyebrows, "Sorry. I would have handed you the phone, but something didn't feel right. It was someone like a realtor."

"A realtor? What is a realtor doing calling me this late?"

"They're wondering how much it'll take to break your lease. I said you weren't interested. Hopefully that's not out of line," he added as he handed her the phone. She checked the number to see an out of state area code.

"Break my lease?" She stared at the number willing it to reveal all. "At my apartment?"

"No," Darius said, "at your shop."

## CHAPTER THIRTEEN

Charlotte had gone home refreshed from the bar but disturbed by the phone call. She had a sinking suspicion it had something to do with that farmers market guy from the other day. If he was making a move on their landlord's property as well, it would mean they'd be out on the street. As bad as their business was doing, she and Faith did not deserve to be shut down. The future of their business had to stay in their control.

Monday morning, she finally got to sleep in but wondered if this would become a regular thing or not. She'd been so flustered after Darius gave her the message, she hadn't asked if he wanted her help the following weekend, as well. She'd also been so worried about the call, she wondered if she could moonlight on weekends at all, or should she focus entirely on protecting Faye's Fortunes.

At eleven, she went out and grabbed coffee for herself and Faith and drove through Fallstaff to their little shop. Although their small town was aging, and was barely a pit stop for wayward travelers, she loved its charm. She didn't want her business to shut down and force them to leave. Although there may be more opportunity for their magical gifts in Jefferson City or even St. Louis, Fallstaff was their home.

By the time she'd pulled her car into small lot behind her shop, she'd decided to call Darius and end it. She would thank him for letting her bartend and make some extra cash, but she needed to focus on building her own business and saving her little village from developers.

His phone went directly to voicemail, which meant it was either off or he was on another call and had deflected her.

*It's fine*, she told herself, he didn't owe her a conversation. She didn't leave a message.

Instead, she texted him:

```
Thanks for the work this weekend. I hope
that kickstart continues to light up your
business! I think its best if I stay in
Fallstaff to light up my business now!
```

In case the exclamation points weren't positive enough, she added a lightbulb emoji to make the text as casual as possible. As soon as she hit send, she felt lonely again.

She grabbed the coffees and headed into her shop.

## CHAPTER FOURTEEN

There were no Reiki customers on Monday or Tuesday. One walk-in customer wanted a short massage of twenty minutes while she waited for a pedicure appointment down the street, but all Charlotte could charge for that was twenty bucks. She spent the rest of the days answering calls from the property management company, creditors, and even Faith's landlord at her apartment, who'd told Charlie to pass on a message to Faith that her electricity was about to be shut off.

Charlotte called Faith's electric company and paid them a hundred bucks of her own money to keep her friend's power on for another couple of weeks. She didn't bother telling Faith what she'd done. She didn't want her to be embarrassed.

Late Tuesday afternoon, Sloane called to thank her for the Jefferson project.

For a moment Charlotte had no idea what she was talking about and she wondered if Sloane's psychoses had started to cause delusions in herself as well.

Then she remembered that Darius was having money troubles, and she'd recommended Sloane to him in passing. She hadn't left him any details, however, so he must have done some digging to find the info - a thought that gave Charlotte a warm feeling inside. She only wished she could afford to hire Sloane for Faye's Fortunes, as well.

"It's no problem at all Slo. Word of mouth gets the work!"

*as does leaving your house, but oh well.*

"I have to go, Charlie."

Charlie could hear the Sloane tinkering with her metal blinds, and figured she'd seen something lurking about in the outside world. Most likely a cat or someone walking their dog.

"You okay?"

"It's nothing, just neighborhood weirdness," laughed Sloane.

Charlie could sense a fear behind the chuckle, though. "Do you need me to come over this week?"

Sloane was quiet for a moment. Charlie figured she was weighing whether to ask her to drive out there or not.

Sloane finally spoke again, "No no, it's fine."

Charlotte sighed.

Faith came into the back room, rubbing her forehead from a distressing reading she'd finished for a high school girl. She spotted Charlotte on the phone and looked at her with concern. It was suspicious anytime either of them had a phone call.

"I might be able to pop over to the city this weekend again," Charlie said. Truthfully, she just wanted any excuse to drive through to St. Louis to see Darius again. Ending their communication via text had been a terrible idea, made even more terrible when he hadn't responded to it!

She mouthed *Sloane* to Faith, who nodded and sat down at the makeup chair.

A few gracious thanks and no-problems were shared with Sloane, and Charlotte hung up.

"You've been in the city a lot," said Faith. It didn't sound accusatory, but Charlie started to feel a twinge of guilt creep across her upper back. She pulled her shoulders up and shook it out.

"It's just my old high school friend," she said.

"The agoraphobe."

When Sloane's psychosis was put into a word like that, Charlotte truly realized the seriousness of it.

"Yeah," she agreed.

Faith smiled, "bring one of my Tarot decks with you and do a reading for her. You should practice."

Charlotte almost asked Faith if she wanted to come do a reading for Sloane, but she stopped herself. She wanted to visit Darius's bar by herself one last time, without having to explain it to Faith.

Faith stared at her in the mirror as though she'd been thinking with her mouth open. She may have been.

Charlotte asked carefully, "Do you want to come do a reading for her yourself?"

"No," Faith said quickly, "you and I see enough of each other during the days. You should get the weekend to yourself. Plus," Faith's eyes took a wicked turn. "I sense there is something you're not sharing with me, and I can tell it's important to you. So, keep it a secret for now."

"You're far too good at this psychic stuff," said Charlotte, "Why don't we have more customers already?"

# CHAPTER FIFTEEN

Wednesday morning, after a fitful night worrying about money, schedules, Sloane's psychoses, and Faith's eviction, Charlotte arrived at work two hours early. The sidewalk was still a mess, so she took the opportunity to sweep the glass stones and crushed cement off to the side of their entrance again. Anything they could do to draw some positive energy into their metaphysical shop was good.

An energy she did *not* want to draw into her shop was that of Pete, the weird developer dude from across the road. But he spotted her and jogged across the roadway, welcoming himself into her personal space all the same.

Just the idea of him was uncomfortable. She tucked her body toward her shop door as if to gain protection from the crystals she had within.

"Have you given any more thought to joining me at the market?"

"You didn't offer it as a thought," Charlotte rolled her eyes "more like you insinuated that it was happening. I'm good here though. So, no thank you."

"You're good? Really?" Once again, he stepped back and looked from Charlotte's shop past all the empty storefronts in between her and the salon at the other end of the plaza. "Really?" he asked again.

"Really," Charlotte insisted, forgoing the last bit of sweeping and backing up through her shop door.

"Because I haven't seen much business walking in and out of these doors," he waved at the store she was backing into. His face turned from pleasant to menacing in a flash, but it disappeared again.

Charlotte didn't like how he made her feel.

At the last minute, rather than open the shop door and enter her store, she realized she wouldn't be safe in a confined area out of public view. Instead, she opted instead to lock up and leave. She left the broom beside the doorframe and locked the door from the outside.

"Ha," Pete laughed. "See? Closing up before you even open for the day."

"Actually," Charlotte pushed passed him and started walking in the direction of the nail salon, "I was just on my way out to grab some refreshments for my partner." She hoped one of the nail technicians was in that early on a Wednesday, just so she'd have some secure company and an excuse to brush off Pete.

Pete didn't follow her. Instead, he backed toward the intersection to cross back over to the empty tire shop. "Think about my proposition to move your store over here," he called from the roadway, "before I make an offer your landlord can't refuse."

"What's that?" Charlotte spun around but continued to back up toward the salon and away from him. "What are you godfathering about?"

"I might just buy this plaza and turn this entire block into a retail and residential complex," he waved his hands around as though he were showing her an imaginary department store.

She had a sudden vision of Fallstaff turning into a boring community of big box stores for Jefferson City.

"But that's almost an hour away," she said quietly.

"What's that?" Pete called as he skipped onto his side of the street.

"Nothing," she said, and watched him walk into the empty tire store. The For Lease sign had been removed sometime in the past day, and she hadn't noticed.

Charlotte peered up and down the road. It seemed ancient, as though cars had disappeared eons before. The empty warehouse he entered was even more derelict without the real estate signs on it. It could certainly use some sprucing up, but not by a shady out-of-state investor. Would the town of Falstaff and her shop's landlord agree to sell these properties to a developer?

"He bugs you too?" a small voice said from behind her.

Startled, Charlotte turned to see the nail salon owner, Alina, standing in her shop entrance smoking a cigarette. Charlotte breathed out and dropped her shoulders, not realizing she'd been as tense as she was. She was so happy to have someone else there with her.

She nodded.

"They won't kick you or me out," Alina blew a smoke ring into the air and dropped the cigarette to the ground. She tapped it out with her toe without even looking at it.

"How do you know?" Charlotte asked.

Alina winked. "Woman's intuition. Come in, I'll get you and Faye some tea."

# CHAPTER SIXTEEN

On Thursday, more creditors called, and Charlotte started ignoring the shop's phone. The sidewalk in front of the store was still destroyed, and from across the road Creepy Pete – a moniker Charlotte and Alina had come up with at the salon - kept eyeing up their property like he was going to sweep it out from under them. Faith still didn't know anything about that part of their business trouble, and Charlotte wanted to keep it that way.

There were no massage clients, either. Just voicemails from bill payees, and Faith talking about buying a coffee machine for the office.

"We can't even afford to answer the phone right now, Faye," Charlie said as she placed feathers in Faith's hair. "I think a coffee machine will have to wait a bit longer."

Faith frowned, and Charlotte saw a flash of guilt sweep across her face.

Charlotte felt bad. She knew Faith wanted to treat them to something nice, but what she'd told her was the truth — they could barely afford to keep the lights on, let alone invest in a coffee machine.

Her cellphone rang on the counter, and she saw Darius' name pop up on the screen. She started toward it but slowed herself. She didn't want to tell Faith she'd worked an extra side gig, that she was waffling over doing it again, or especially that she had a silly crush on a man, so instead she left the phone and hoped he would leave a message.

"I'll try to drum up some business today," Faith said, "I saw the old tire shop across the street was having some repairs done. Maybe I'll go over there and introduce myself to the new owne-"

"-don't," Charlotte said quickly, poking a feather into Faith's skull.

"Ow!" Faith cringed, "Okay, okay, why not?"

"Sorry," Charlotte gently massaged Faith's scalp and felt her friend relax under her touch. "I met the guy yesterday, and he's just really busy," she lied.

The fact was she didn't trust Pete, and he sounded like he was going to try and buy their land and business out from under them, but Charlotte didn't want to worry an already stressed-out Faith. Although they were in business together and everything was shared, it was Faith's name on the billboard and the creditor calls always asked for her first.

Charlotte said, "I'll try to get more business today. You just sit here looking ethereal and divine. I'll pull some customers in for you."

"From where?" Faith was genuinely curious.

*I don't have any idea*, Charlotte thought, but she said, "Doesn't matter, I'm on it!"

# CHAPTER SEVENTEEN

Later that afternoon, she noticed a text from Darius had come in during the morning. She must have had the sound turned off in the hopes of attracting clientele, as she hadn't heard it beep at all.

The message was a simple "What can I do to change your mind?"

She scratched her head, having forgotten what it was a response to, so she opened the phone and saw her text from earlier in the week telling him she wouldn't be visiting his bar anymore.

Just as she was attempting to compose a coherent thought, she heard the jingle of the bells on the shop door. She put the phone down and headed out to the lobby. Faith also approached from her fortune telling room.

At the entrance stood Darius.

"I- what are you doing here?" Charlotte stared into Darius's eyes.

Faith stopped and took in Darius's muscles.

Charlotte shook herself out of her stupor. "It's a massage client. I got this, Faye."

"You must be the mind reader," Darius flashed a bright smile at Faith.

Darius's body, smile, and voice was mesmerizing even for the most professional of people. Charlotte could see Faith start to blush a deep crimson.

"She's a card reader," Charlotte interjected quickly. "Faith, Darius. Darius, Faith."

Faith seemed to wake up out of her flushed confusion, and she curtsied. "Enchanté."

Charlotte felt a twinge of envy, but quickly reminded herself that her best friend was not her competition,

*Plus there's nothing to compete for. This isn't a relationship,* she reminded herself a little too forcefully.

"Why don't we go for a walk, Darius?"

"I'll hold down the fort," Faith said in her mystical voice, as though a thousand spirits were fighting for space in their small shop lobby. Truthfully, there hadn't been much magical energy, nor customers, for quite a while.

Outside, Charlotte tip-toed around the loose sidewalk stones and led Darius along the plaza sidewalk.

"Lots of empty stores here," he noted.

"It's not for lack of trying," Charlotte nodded.

Beside Faye's Fortunes was an abandoned restaurant, the windows boarded up so you couldn't see in anymore. Next to that, she waved at an old display window, where a pile of dusty books lay in a heap. "This used to be a bookstore. That one we just passed with the newspapers in the window was a teriyaki place. It was delicious."

"What happened?"

"Development, mostly. The bigger highway brought small town business into the city. You know how it is."

"I guess," Darius agreed. "I get a lull on weekends because the industry isn't there."

"Last weekend your club was poppin', though," Charlotte smiled.

"That's because of you! And it's why I'm here." Darius took her by the shoulders and turned her to face him. She felt her knees weaken and her skin heat up under his strong fingers. "I need you to come work for me."

"Darius, I-"

"Hey!" a voice shouted from across the street, and Charlotte turned to see Pete crossing the road toward them.

"Oh no, here we go."

Pete gave Darius a few once-overs, as if he was calculating what the odds were who'd win if they got into a fight.

Charlotte rolled her eyes. It felt like she was in the middle of a bizarre alpha male stare-down. "What do you want, Mr. Halton? We're not selling our business, and that's final."

"Oh, you don't have to sell. Once I buy this property from the landlord, you'll be *begging* me to keep you in business. But from what they tell me you might be out on your ass long before then."

"What's going on?" Darius put his hands on his hips.

"That's enough, Mr. Halton," Alina said from the doorway of her nail salon, stubbing out a cigarette. To

Darius, she smiled, "Come inside my shop, you need a manicure."

Charlotte watched a flash of anger cross Pete's face. He didn't enjoy being dismissed.

"Thanks. Charlotte, we can continue our conversation inside," Darius glowered at Pete and put a protective hand on the small of Charlotte's back.

"We were talking too," Pete stood firm, but still at least six feet away and trying desperately to make himself look taller.

If her eyes rolled any further back in her head, Charlotte would have to see a specialist. Both men were being ridiculous.

"Pete," she said, "this is between you and the landlord. Our shop is not moving. Welcome to the neighborhood and goodbye. Alina, I could use a manicure too -"

"-Come right in. Anything for my favorite neighbor."

"I'm your only neighbor," sighed Charlotte, and she led Darius past Pete and into the nail parlor.

# CHAPTER EIGHTEEN

"You still haven't told me what you're doing here," Charlotte said to Darius as they sat side by side at the nail station. Two young women giggled and whispered in Russian to each other as they stole glances at Darius's muscular forearms. They seemed to be arguing over who would get to work on his nails. When Charlotte picked her seat, she could tell the tech working on her nails was envious of her peer.

For a moment she wondered if they were saying cruel things about her. Suddenly, a voice, clear as day, resounded in her head. "Let the ladies have their fun."

She realized it was her own inner voice and she straightened in surprise.

"You okay?" Darius took his hand out of the nail technician's grasp, and he reached toward Charlotte.

"Yes, yes I'm fine. Sorry about that. I don't know what came over me just then."

But she did know. She'd felt a surge of magical energy, the same energy she'd used ages ago when she'd first gotten into Reiki and opened the shop with Faye. She'd felt a bit of it at the bar the previous weekend, and again when Darius had called the other day, but this was bolder. This sense that she knew exactly what was happening and what it meant, was completely different.

"I have to get back to the shop," Charlotte said.

"You need to let your nails dry," Alina ordered from behind them. She brought out a tray of teas and put them between Darius and Charlotte. Darius sipped his and placed his other hand under the drying lamp.

"It can wait, can't it? It's lunch hour," Darius said, "and to answer your question, I'm here for *you*."

"What?"

"The question you asked when we first sat down. What am I here for? I'm here to see you!"

If this were any other man, she might almost feel smothered. Something about Darius made her comfortable instead. She felt alive when he was near her.

Comfort didn't stop the curiosity. "I see. So, you came out this crazy long way just to try and pull me back to your pub tonight?"

"Well, that, and my Dad was coming out here for another delivery. I wanted to make sure-"

"He didn't run over anymore shop sidewalks?"

"Exactly."

"Where is he now?" Charlotte looked out the store window, but the street was quiet, save for some construction crews moving stuff around in the tire shop across the road.

"He's helping a nice old woman move her stuff out of her house. He said he'd be awhile and that he didn't need any help." Darius waved his fingers in the air. "I think he sensed I needed my nails done."

Darius's fingers had been painted clear, but still he blew on them as though they were a Mondrian.

Charlotte laughed. "They do look much better than they did before." she kept her hands squarely in the drying lamp to stop herself from touching him. "Those cases of cheap whiskey weren't doing your cuticles any favors."

"I suppose if you're not coming to help me lift the cases anymore, I'll have to come to this nail salon more often."

"Only if you pick a color next time," Alina said behind them.

Both Charlotte and Darius chuckled and stared down at their nails, throwing glances at each other.

#

As they stood from their seats and made their way to the front of the nail salon, Charlotte felt a sense of relief wash over her. She was certain the coast was clear of Pete, and that it was safe to return to her shop.

At the register, Darius asked Alina, "How much do I owe you for our fancy digits?" He wiggled his fingers and then reached for his wallet.

"You'll pay me next time," she said, and waved them toward the door.

"Are you sure? What about tips?" Charlotte looked back at the two techs, who were still giggling and watching Darius.

"It's no trouble. They appreciate having some business today."

Darius pushed a twenty into Alina's hands, "and we appreciate the excuse not to talk to that Pete guy. Please, take it for them."

Alina graciously accepted the bill and opened her till to split it up for the technicians.

Charlotte felt sad for the salon. She wondered if they were struggling with paying the plaza's landlord, too.

As if reading her mind, Alina asked, "You don't have anyone bothering you about rent, right?"

"I mean, there are phone calls," Charlotte said.

Alina scowled. "Phone calls? From who?"

"The property management company, realtors, that sort of thing."

"On mudak!"

One of the techs gasped at Alina's expression and whispered something to the other. They pointed and chortled intensely. Alina shushed them but blushed at her expletive.

Charlotte didn't bother asking what Alina had uttered. The salon's happy vibe was enough to fill her with joy.

"Thank you again, Alina, this manicure was refreshing. I wish you good business today."

"From a witch, that means a great deal," the woman beamed at them as Darius held the door for Charlotte.

Out on the sidewalk Charlotte whispered, "Did she just call me a witch?"

Darius laughed.

As they started walking back toward Faye's Fortunes, they heard a cargo truck roll up beside them and honk.

"Hey Darius," Mark called from the window. "You ready to head back to the city?"

"You're done already, Dad?"

"Yeah, the lady said she wasn't quite done going through all of her things. We'll be back again next week to get the rest of it. I got a half a truckload ready, though." Mark stepped down from the cabin and came around the front. To Charlotte he said, "Hello miss, I hope you're well."

She could sense he was nervous and intimidated. His eyes darted to the still-busted sidewalk in front of her shop.

"Hi," she beamed. "Everything is all good." She reached for his shoulder and willed her palm to send waves of relaxing energy into him. It seemed to work, and his embarrassment appeared to shift into gratitude.

"I guess I'd better go," Darius stepped from one foot to the other as though he didn't know whether to hug her or head for the truck.

She didn't quite know, either. She felt the skin on her face warm.

Mark coughed, "Okay then, let's get on the road." As he turned back toward the front of the truck, he added "looks like we'll be back next week for sure."

Darius nodded and made a small, awkward wave, then climbed into his side of the truck. Charlotte felt a chill from where his body had left her aura again. She shook it off and smiled.

"I hope business is booming for you this weekend," Darius called from the truck.

"And yours too," Charlotte waved. Although she felt sad that they were several hours away from each other, she did mean it. She wanted his bar to succeed on its own, without her.

# CHAPTER NINETEEN

Friday morning, Charlotte fumbled through drawers trying to find feathers to stick in Faith's hair, hoping to magically transform her best friend into the savvy businesswoman and psychic that she was.

"Who was that dreamy guy yesterday?" Faith asked, curious. "Has Charlie finally got a little something-something on the side?"

Charlotte frowned and stared into a drawer. Although she was blushing on the inside, she didn't want to project a relationship that wasn't viable. *Is it even a relationship?* She didn't want to pretend or hope.

"A massage customer," she lied.

Before Faith could inquire about how much money she may have pulled in yesterday, Charlotte added quickly "- and not a very lucrative one at that."

"We can't keep giving discounts and freebies," Faith lamented.

"I'd be happy to charge full price if we could get more wallets in the front door," Charlotte slammed a drawer a little too hard.

Faith jumped. Charlotte realized she was being overreactive in order to hide her feelings.

"I'm sorry," she calmed herself. "I'm just as frustrated as you are."

"No, I'm the one who's sorry, Charlie. You're the one with actual, regular clients. I should be the one busting ass to get us more business while you're working."

"You're doing enough. We both are," Charlotte sighed.

To herself she added, *I'm even moonlighting at a bar nearly three hours away.*

Faith drew her out of her head when she said, "we could move the shop to Jefferson City."

Charlotte wondered if her psychic friend was reading her mind. Had she mentally heard Charlotte talk about moonlighting in that direction?

Faith continued, "I think this small town just can't handle a divination and alternative health store."

Charlotte relaxed. It was a business discussion, not a psychic premonition. She thought about it some more and, although the idea did excite her immensely - she'd be able to visit with Sloane more often, work nights at the bar with Darius, and still get enough sleep to work a full day at the shop with her best friend the next day - moving to Jefferson City was out of the question for their little store.

She pushed a half-broken feather into Faith's head and jeered, "Oh yeah, with what money would we use to relocate a store?"

The shop door chimed and Faith, now transformed into majestic Faye, floated out of the back office. "Ah, our esteemed client awaits."

Charlotte smiled until she was safely out of view, but then her shoulders fell. It would be a dream to work closer to Darius, but her business was here, her apartment was here, and her best friend was here.

She heard a commotion out in the lobby, it seemed Faith's crush had appeared. Charlotte tried to stay out of sight and admitted to herself that a bit of envy had started to take over in her head. Faith was developing relationships with the people in Fallstaff, including this new guy Jasper, and although Charlotte was working hard and trying to drum up business, her heart was in a city almost three hours away, and she didn't have time to get there and back and still save her massage practice.

She stared at herself in the makeup mirror and tried desperately to find the energy needed to be a fantastic Reiki practitioner. What had Alina called her the other day? A witch? Why did she not feel it now? Why did she feel it *then*?

Her shoulder twitched. In the mirror, she watched the wisdom creep across her face before her body knew the truth. She had a sudden, tiny flash of insight as to what was happening. She *was* magic, but not when she was alone. All the energy she felt and all the magic she could concoct only happened when Darius was nearby.

Having a crush on someone was the enchantment that inspired her to be a better healer.

She heard the shop door slam and a coldness fell over the office as Faith flew through the door and sobbed into her arms. "Did you hear all that?"

"I didn't need to hear it, hon. I felt it," Charlotte lied.

She held her friend while she wept, but inside she'd just had an amazing revelation.

# CHAPTER TWENTY

The sidewalk was fixed later that afternoon, and Faith's sobbing breakdown appeared to have brought back her psychic energy with it. Charlotte watched her make predictions for the construction crew out front, and her belief in herself seemed to return.

Charlotte was envious. Nothing seemed to bring back her healing powers except for Darius, "and he's hours away," she lamented to no one as she collected her bags to go home for the evening.

"Who?" Faith asked as she watched the sidewalk construction crew pack up for the day.

"Huh?" Charlotte hadn't realized she'd been talking to herself. "No one, it's not important."

She felt Faith staring at her.

"You know, Charlie," Faith said, unwrapping a crystal ball from its packaging and rubbing her hands over it. "I've noticed your reiki healing energy seems to ebb and flow depending on the day."

"Careful with those powers that are coming back to you, Faye Faye. You're not allowed to use them on me."

"I can't help it," laughed Faith, "It's so easy to make predictions when you can sense that someone is in love."

"I'm not in love!" Charlotte grabbed a feather hairpin and launched it at Faith. It fluttered haphazardly through the air and fell into a pile on the floor, pointing toward the door.

Faith laughed. "I'll stop making predictions about you, but I have one final thing to say."

Charlotte eyed her suspiciously.

"I can sense there is somewhere you want to be tonight. Maybe it's your friend Sloane's house," Faith tilted an eyebrow then shook her head. "Or maybe not. I won't read into that."

Faith opened the door and ushered Charlotte toward it. "Why don't you leave now so you can make the trek, then come in late tomorrow morning."

Charlotte had already told Darius she couldn't commute this far anymore. She scrambled for an excuse. "Who will bring you your coffee tomorrow?"

Faith laughed. "Do you think that's all I use you for?"

"Actually, sometimes." Charlotte approached the door.

Faith all but pushed her out. "I'll bring *you* a coffee. You're going to need it after your commute to see that cute guy."

"Hey," Charlotte said as she scrambled out of the shop, trying to avoid the freshly poured concrete. "You promised no more psychic predictions about my love life."

"Sure, Charlie. But I didn't promise not to make predictions about *his*!" Faith laughed and shut the door behind her.

# CHAPTER TWENTY-ONE

The drive to St. Louis seemed shorter than usual. Charlotte felt she had time to stop in and check Sloane's mail for her. As usual, her friend had a million excuses as to why she hadn't checked it in a week.

"I can't trust the new neighbors that are moving in," Sloane whispered from behind the front door. She shut it quickly after Charlotte was through, as though the air was a poison ready to murder both of them.

Charlotte rolled her eyes and didn't bother removing her shoes. She wanted to continue to Darius's bar and get there while it was still reasonably light outside.

"Hey," Sloane said, "I wanted to thank you again for that accounting business you sent my way."

Charlotte was focused on the heavy stack of mail, "Huh, which?"

"That guy with the bar. His savings are in great shape, but his business was flopping a little bit. It's been refreshing for my brain to help him leverage a few different things so he can grow."

Charlotte tried to feign nonchalance, "Oh, Darius. Right. Well, you're the best finance person I know, Slo."

Sloane looked at her feet and waved the notion away.

Charlotte continued, "I only wish we could use you at Faye's Fortune. We're having some cash flow problems ourselves."

Sloane smiled, "I'm always happy to help out however I can. You've done more than enough for me."

"I don't take freebies," Charlotte smiled. Then she nodded toward the door behind her, "I do need to hit the road before it gets too late. Do you want your key back?" She held the mail key out for Sloane.

"Just keep it," Sloane said.

What she left unsaid was *you're the only one who checks my mailbox anyway.*

"I'll make you a copy," Charlotte backed toward the door. "I have a good feeling about you. I think you'll need a second mail key soon."

Sloane eyed her curiously. "Something is different about you, Charlie. Are your mystical gifts coming back?"

Charlotte knew they were, but Darius was the reason, and she needed to go see him to keep her magic charged, as it were. She put her hand on the doorknob and waited to open it. Her friend had to recuse herself from the front hall.

#

The drive toward St. Louis was a lot slower than it had been into Jefferson City. None of the drivers on the road seemed to know where they were going. It was like driving behind a thousand of Mark's moving trucks. Charlotte laughed at the thought.

By the time she rolled into the industrial lot and under the beaming neon sign, it was already ten o'clock at night. She hoped Darius's business had picked up, for his own sake.

When she opened the door, she was pleased to see the turnout. Perry was at the bar and a few others were milling around.

Darius was pulling bottles down from the shelves and putting them in a box behind the bar.

At the sound of the door chime, Perry looked up from his dwindling whiskey glass. "It's my lady again!"

"Hi Perry," Charlotte smiled.

Darius shot up from behind the bar. "What are you doing here?"

"She came to see me." Perry beamed.

"Nobody wants to see you, you bum," another bar visitor shouted.

Charlotte wished she'd come up with an excuse to be there, but the truth was she just wanted to see him. "I had to get Sloane's mail, so-"

Darius crinkled a brow "So you drove an extra hour further just to see me?"

"Me!" Perry yelled and slammed his glass down on the bar.

"Hour and a half, but yeah." Charlotte felt her face flush. She rounded the bar and took Perry's glass from him. She held it up for Darius and tried to mentally ask *can he have another?*

Darius seemed to read her mind and nodded. She poured the drink.

Perry sat back in his chair and looked utterly pleased with himself. The other bar patrons chuckled at him.

It was then that Charlotte saw the boxes of booze on the floor and the partially empty shelves. She looked around at the pub. A group was drinking heavily and playing pool in the back corner, and there were a few people at the bar - although that included Perry who rarely paid - but it didn't seem dead at all.

She grew concerned and waved at the boxes, "I know business was a little slow, but is it so bad you have to close up?"

"No! Business is great," Darius insisted, "even better whenever you're here." He reached for her, but dropped his hand, then backed away, pulling more bottles down off the shelf.

"Then what are you doing?"

"Oh, this?" Darius seemed at a loss for words. "Just taking inventory."

Charlotte sensed he was lying and tried to extract info out of him. "Sloane said things were pretty good for you right now."

From behind her, Charlotte heard "Pretty good? It's great!"

She turned to see Mark coming out of the back office.

He came around the bar and gave Charlotte a hug. Although she wished it was from Darius, she enjoyed a big bear hug from his old man.

Darius frowned. She wondered if he wished he'd hugged her, too.

Charlotte started to ask Mark, "Does this mean-"

"-that I'm quitting the delivery driver business? Hell yes!"

"Thank goodness. I guess I owe Sloane one, don't I?"

"She's really helped me out a lot." Darius nodded. "I hope to meet her in person someday."

"Ha, doubtful -" Charlotte started, but left the rest unsaid.

#

Mark, Darius, and Charlotte worked the bar together for an hour or two, and as business slowed in the industrial park, the bar filled up and came alive.

Perry stumbled away into the night, but as if by magic he was replaced with actual paying customers, many of them.

Eventually, the boxes of booze behind the bar became an obstacle for the three bartenders to fumble around.

"Why don't you two carry some of these boxes into the back," Mark asked. "This place is jumping, and we need more room to work here."

"We also need more booze here," Charlotte eyed the boxes as she picked one up. Darius grabbed two more and led the way toward the back room.

When they were safely out of view from the crowd, she asked, "D'you wanna tell me what's going on here?"

Darius continued into the office and put his two boxes on the floor beside the desk. In the room were even more boxes of liquor loaded up as though they'd just been taken off a palette.

"Okay, this is whack," Charlotte said, staring at the haul, "You have enough booze stored back here for a whole other bar."

At this, Darius chuckled. "That's the dream, isn't it?"

Charlotte eyed him.

"I promise, this will all make sense." He took the heavy box from Charlotte, and she relaxed her shoulders.

Darius saw this action and placed his hand on her arm. She immediately felt a bolt of lightning power through her body when he touched her.

"It's so good to see you," he said in a half whisper, as though his mouth had gone dry.

"It's good to see you too," she murmured, stomach fluttering like a teenager falling in lust for the first time.

He moved his face closer. Before his lips touched hers, he stared deeply into her eyes, pausing for consent.

She nodded, and he worshipped her with his soft lips.

It felt like a millennium passed before they came up for air, but she still wanted more. When he pulled his mouth away from hers, it left her bereft of something vital. Her entire body felt electric.

"I've wanted to do that for a long time," he said under his breath.

"Hmm-mm," was all she could get out.

He seemed lost for a moment and stepped back, which only made her want him more.

"There's something else I've wanted to do for a long time," Charlotte found herself saying.

"Oh yeah, what's that?"

Before she could stop herself, and before she let the time and distance break them apart again, she reached her arms around his neck and hoisted her legs up around his waist. He grabbed her backside and pressed her entire body into his. While he held her, she tore off his shirt and hers, then dove back in to kiss him some more.

"Yes," he growled into her, and lowered her down onto the desk. He groaned in agony and delight.

"Is your arm okay," she shuddered below him, worried she'd been too aggressive.

"My entire body is okay, now that my energy healer is here." He tore off the rest of their clothes as easily as if they were made of paper.

# CHAPTER TWENTY-TWO

Although they'd tried to take their time, the back office of a pub was not the most romantic location for a first time, so Charlotte had gone into it knowing full well it wasn't going to be amazing. Yet even a quickie had rejuvenated her mind, body, and spirit. She felt like she could take on the world.

"I guess traveling wouldn't be so bad," she muttered to herself as she pulled her jeans back on.

"Hmm?" Darius hummed dreamily, visibly flustered by the inside-out condition of his t-shirt.

Charlotte laughed at him, "here." She took the t-shirt and in one motion flipped it right-side out. She held the neck open for his head and watched him bend into it.

"You didn't groan," she said as he stuck an arm through the tee.

"You're magic," he pulled the shirt over the other arm and down his glistening body. He half-growled, "I don't know what you did to me."

"I know what I did to you," she winked and ran her hands over his chest, feigning flattening the wrinkles out of his t-shirt, but in actuality she only wanted to touch him some more.

"No," he said and took her face in his hands. He stared into her eyes, "you really are an energy healer. Everything you touch seems to mend itself."

"Only when you're near me," she told him. She pulled back from him, adjusted her sweater over her body, and slipped back into her shoes. "When you visited that first day and then again yesterday, that was when my gift was the strongest. Your energy is my power source."

She leaned forward to kiss him on the cheek, then wiped away a remainder of lipstick - not that there was much left after their tryst. "Truth be told," she admitted, "I came here to suck up more of it so I can work better tomorrow."

"You can suck up more of me any time," he growled into her neck and lifted her into a high hug.

She squealed, "You're welcome to drop by Fallstaff for a massage anytime. I certainly wouldn't mind some of this magic every day."

"I think we can make that possible," Darius laughed, set her down, and opened the door for her.

The booming noises of the pub drowned her out as she asked, "but how?"

## CHAPTER TWENTY-THREE

If Mark knew what they'd done he didn't say anything, although he did give the pair of them sly smiles throughout the evening. The three bartenders worked efficiently for the rest of the night, the two men each taking an end of the bar, and Charlotte making the rounds with a drink tray.

Whenever they were near each other, Charlotte and Darius couldn't help but touch. He would tap her backside while she was pouring drinks, or she'd put a stabilizing hand on his back while he reached for a high bottle. When she was out working the floor, they'd wink at each other.

A steady stream of truckers and warehouse workers came and went, and the evening flew by quickly. When Charlotte finally had a chance to check the clock it was already 1:30am.

"Shit," she said into the cash register.

"What's wrong," Darius came over and put an arm around her shoulders.

She melted into him as she ran a credit card through the machine. "I just didn't realize how late it was. I need to start heading home. Saturdays are usually our busiest days at the shop."

"Wow," Darius had looked at the clock as well. "Luckily, since it's late it shouldn't take you as long to get home."

"Yeah, luckily," Charlotte sighed. She handed the credit card back to the customer and grabbed her handbag from under the bar.

"Why don't you stay the night here in St. Louis? I don't have anything in the morning. I could come with you for the ride," Darius suggested.

"No, no" she waved a hand around the bar. "You still have so many customers tonight, and I don't want one of us to be stuck without a car. Your Dad needs you here. I'll be alright."

"Will you-"

"I should-"

They'd tried to speak at the same time. Both looked down at their feet and shuffled them.

"I probably need sleep tomorrow night, so I can't come back this weekend," Charlotte lamented as Darius walked her to the pub door.

Darius seemed confident when he said, "I'll see you next week, then."

"Maybe," Charlotte gave him a quick peck on the lips and headed to her car. "Maybe not," she whispered to no one.

## CHAPTER TWENTY-FOUR

On Saturday morning there was a lineup around the shop corner. A myriad of customers were waiting to get in and experience Faye's magic. Charlotte was elated that Faye's psychic gift had returned, because it meant more business for herself, as well.

After her fun night with Darius - both in the bar and in his back office - she was feeling extra energetic, as though she could heal anything in anyone. She started with a strong female construction worker who looked desperate to relax.

"You're magic," the customer groaned five minutes into the massage. Charlotte had barely even touched her, but she could sense all her sore joints and muscle knots before the woman had even laid down. Charlotte's fingers tingled before touching the woman's skin, and what felt like calming energy flowed between them for the entire session.

If the customers in the lobby were becoming unruly, the woman didn't seem to notice, and she melted into Charlotte's touch.

After the massage, when the customer was back in her construction gear, she pulled her hair back into a stringy, split-ended pony and noticed something on a high shelf. She asked, "what's that rock?"

Charlotte followed her finger toward a dusty crystal. "That's Howlite. In natural healing it's used for pain relief, calming energy, and reinvigorating one's energy."

The woman continued to stare at the stone's veining colors of black and white. "I'll take it!"

"Seriously, you want to buy my gemstone?"

"I may be a tough-looking tradeswoman, but I know what makes me feel good," the woman insisted. "Name your price."

Even Charlotte's untouched crystals sparkled as though their strength had been restored. After the woman left the massage room, she brought more of her stones down from the high shelves and unpacked some from their boxes to put on display. If one customer was willing to buy a rock on psychic energy alone, maybe others would, as well.

It worked, too. That entire day customers came in, felt immediately re-energized, and bought lotions and crystals so they could continue the magical feeling all the way home.

Charlotte's pockets continued to fill, but by the end of the day her heart was emptying.

She knew her magic was there only because Darius had brought it out of her the night before. When she thought of him she felt alive, invigorated, renewed, and full of love energy that she could pass on to her clients. But as time passed and she was separated from him, the void grew again. Darius's bar in St. Louis was too far for a hardworking smalltown shopkeeper to visit every night. She couldn't maintain a long-distance side job or even a fleeting romance, but she also knew that if she went too long without seeing him, she'd lose her gift and business would slow again.

She was literally between a rock and a hard place - her crystals were the rocks, and the hard place was Darius's body. She needed both to keep going.

## CHAPTER TWENTY-FIVE

On Sunday, one of Faith's neighbors gave Charlie fresh sheets and even more crystals. Charlotte was gracious and amazed. While carrying the box of fun new stuff to her shop, she said out loud, "It's true what they say - what you give out into the world, you get back three-fold."

From somewhere ahead of the large box, she heard "Who says that? The witches?"

Her heart skipped at Darius's voice.

"What are you doing here," she asked, looking up and down the street for Mark's truck.

"You ask me that a lot," Darius laughed. Sensing what she was looking for, he said "Dad's not here, he's selling his truck. A moving truck career was a bad idea."

Charlotte chuckled and looked sheepishly down at her now-fixed sidewalk.

Darius added, "I'm out here on my own today. Need help?"

He reached his hand out for the boxes, but she shook her head and continued toward the shop. "You can get this door for me. You don't need any more strain on your frozen shoulder."

"You fixed that, remember," he said, walking beside her toward the shop entrance. With the sidewalk fixed again, the entire atmosphere of the shop corner felt vibrant and energetic.

Charlie smiled and felt her face flush as they headed inside. She was with her man, she was at her store, and everything just felt right. She hated that it was barely a love affair, at best. It couldn't last this way.

"You never told me why you're in town again," she said as he closed the shop door behind her.

Once inside, Darius did take the box from her, only so he could set it down on a counter. Then he held her hands in his and said, "I'm here on a mission."

"What mission is that?" she reached her chin up for a kiss.

"A couple of things," he said, giving her a quick smooch. "One," he kissed her lightly again, "I'm checking out the neighborhood."

She raised an eyebrow but didn't speak lest she miss out on another quick kiss.

"Two," he pecked her cheek, "someone said she'd give me a massage if I ever found myself in her town."

He pulled back and winked at her.

She swatted at him playfully, "I think you're using your sexy wiles to trick me into offering you freebies."

"It's true," he grabbed her hands, "I'm a siren calling you."

"I knew it! No wonder I'm tempted to drive out to the big city every night. I need to sleep and work, you know."

"Oh, I know. Now show me your massage studio."

The shop wouldn't open for another hour or so, and Charlotte knew Faith was busy with her own plans that morning, so she locked the shop door, shut the curtains, and in the sultry ambiance she led Darius to her massage room. She wondered how much healing massage would actually happen, as she could barely keep her hands to herself.

When he saw the space, his eyes lit up. "It's beautiful."

"It's just like any old massage room," she tried to see what he was looking at.

"No, it's magic," he said. "It's inspiring and relaxing. I already feel a million times healthier."

Charlotte shuffled her feet and smiled weakly, "Thanks, I try."

"More people need to know about this place," Darius said, eying some amethyst that sparkled in the morning light. "Now strip."

"Huh wut?"

"You heard me." He spun around to face her. "I used to be a masseuse myself, you know."

Charlotte was caught off guard. "You want to massage…me?"

"Come on," Darius said, lifting her shirt over her shoulders. "When was the last time you had a moment to just chill?"

"I mean," Charlotte thought about it and smiled. "About two minutes ago when you were kissing me."

"Come on," Darius pulled the cover back on her massage table. "I mean one hour where you didn't also have unpaid bills, business problems, friend issues, difficult journeys to your boyfriend's place, and questionable realtors calling you at all hours."

Charlotte sat on the bed and swung her legs under the covers he held for her. "Wait a minute," she started, unbuttoning her pants.

"What?" He looked away, like a professional, although he didn't have to.

"Did you just call yourself my boyfriend?"

Darius laughed. "Lady, I don't put out for just anyone. Now, take the rest of your clothes off."

#

Despite the sexy demand, Darius didn't start any funny business at all. This would otherwise be disappointing except that instead, for an entire hour, he massaged her body like a baker kneading his finest bread. She felt electric, but also so relaxed she fell asleep toward the end.

"Hey," he whispered to her after he was done.

"Mmmm," Charlotte groaned, and surprised herself by waking up. "Why didn't you take advantage of me while I was out?"

"I admit it's hard not to." He rubbed the lotion off his hands with a towel. With a smug flair he added, "but I'm a professional."

"I'm a professional too, and I certainly wouldn't be able to resist *your* body," Charlotte teased, reaching a hand down from the bed to grab his butt.

Darius faked a gasp, "Excuse me miss, this is a business!" He winked at her and left the room, allowing her to get back into her clothes in private.

*He doesn't need to leave*, she thought. He'd seen and felt her whole naked body the previous evening. Yet something about his professionalism was comforting. She could tell he had at one point in his life been a masseuse. Despite his strong muscles he was gentle, smooth, knew where to find knots and how to get them out without hurting her, and how to revive her soul for the day.

She felt alive, awake, and ready for another long day of work.

Fully dressed, she walked out into the lobby and found Darius holding a green gemstone he'd found on a shelf.

"It's Aventurine," she told him, putting a hand around his back.

"I could use an adventurine," he groaned down at her, kissing the top of her head.

"A-venturine. There's no 'd'." She took the rock from him and held it up under the light, so tiny specs of silver and gold shone through the light green. "It's good for business success, instilling hard work, and attracting clients."

"I'll buy it!" Darius put the rock on the counter, "I need all the business luck I can get."

Charlotte laughed, "your business is doing fine now, you just needed to lighten it up." She picked up the aventurine and stuck it in the front pocket of his jeans, using the opportunity to tickle his hip and pull herself closer to him for a kiss. "The gemstone is on the house for that miraculous massage. Take it back to St. Louis with you, I insist."

"Okay." He stared down into her eyes as his mouth grazed hers. "But only because I have a big project on the horizon and need some luck."

Charlotte started, "What proj-"

The front door chimed, and Faith floated inside, smiling in love. Behind her, her new partner Jasper waved at someone outside and followed her into the shop.

"Charlie, you're here, thank goodness," Faith breathed. "We've got to get to work!"

"What are you talking about?" Charlotte moved away from Darius too quickly. Her heart almost started yearning for him like he was three hours away again.

"I'm not sure. I guess it must be homecoming season or something, because outside is a lineup of teens wondering if their dreams will come true, and their anxious parents wanting to relax."

Charlotte's jaw dropped. "Another busy day? How is that possible?"

But she knew how it was possible. Whenever she was near Darius, business became magic. "You're some sort of magnet for customers," she whispered to him.

"It's all you, Charlie" Darius hummed into her ear and gave her a quick kiss on the cheek. "I have to run; I have a meeting with my new landlord."

"Your what?"

"Come on, Charlotte! We need to get ready," Faith blew Jasper a kiss and he went back out into the fray. When Faith passed by Darius on her way to the back office, she stopped, "You must be the tall drink of water occupying my friend's head all the time."

"Darius." He chuckled and held out a hand for her.

Faith blushed at his strength, and when her palm met his, her eyes glazed over for a brief second. She made a funny half-giggle noise. "I'm Faith. I can't wait to hear all about your new business."

"How'd you know-?" Darius eyed her. "Oh right, you're the psychic."

"What new business?" Charlotte glared at each of them.

"I'll let you know in a bit," Darius kissed Charlotte on the forehead and dashed for the door. "My landlord has already put the kettle on!"

# CHAPTER TWENTY-SIX

For the second day in a row, business was booming. For the wide-eyed teens, Faith predicted amazing and devastating news, but all of it was in a way that was positive, uplifting, and made everyone leave her fortune room in a good mood. At the same time, Charlotte had a steady stream of anxious parents needing a relaxing shoulder massage or some crystals for good luck.

One woman requested foot reflexology - or a psychic prediction based on the shape of her feet - but Charlotte figured her poor tootsies were bent out of shape from the too small stilettos she was wearing. Charlotte rubbed the knots out of her arches and gently suggested that her feet's psychic prediction was to opt for sandals, instead.

Every customer left pleased, and Charlotte and Faith reveled in both the busyness and the fresh cash in their till.

"It's him, you know," Charlotte said as she slumped in a chair in the back office.

"I know." Faith touched up her makeup in the mirror. "Your business has improved because you've fallen in love. I know exactly what that's like."

Charlotte flinched at the word 'love,' but Faith was right. This kind of magic didn't just happen after a one-nighter. Charlotte had experienced enough of those in her life to recognize that this was different.

She seemed to say all these things without speaking, but she knew Faith understood.

"But you're lucky," Charlotte finally said out loud, as she opened and closed the cash register. It was if she was mesmerized that it had bills in it. "Your new love works right here in town so you can see him all the time. I can't drive to St. Louis and back every night just to keep my mojo fires burning. It's unsustainable!"

Faith fluffed the feathers in her hair and walked halfway out the office door. "Thank goodness you won't have to do that anymore."

Just as Faith nodded her head toward the lobby, the door chime sounded.

"I will never understand how you do that," Charlotte shook her head and followed Faith out into the shop. Darius stood by the door and beamed, "Paperwork is signed, I got it!"

"I knew it." Faith smiled and headed toward her fortune room.

"Somebody had better fill me in real fast or I'm going to scream," Charlotte put her hands on her hips.

Darius and Faith laughed, and Faith winked at him.

"Come here," he opened the shop door and beckoned her to follow him out.

She huffed, frustrated but too curious to stand her ground waiting for answers, and went through the door. Outside, she waited for him to show her where to go.

He exited the shop behind her, closed the door, and started down the walkway in the direction of the nail salon. But he had barely taken five steps when he said "Welcome-" he spread his arms wide in front of the empty restaurant next door, "-to Jefferson's Pub, Fallstaff."

Darius pulled a key out of his pocket and opened the door.

"You're renting this space? But how-"

"Your friend Sloane was able to leverage the property in St. Louis." He opened the door and let Charlotte walk in ahead of him. "We're a franchise now, baby!"

The place was dusty, but the magic of the previous restaurant was still there. A paint job, some stain on the bar, and a few updates would be all it took to get the old place running again.

As if reading her mind, Darius offered, "My Dad will run the St. Louis location while I finish the work here. If I work every day and get the liquor permits in line, I should be open within the month."

Charlotte was stunned, but it felt wonderful to be back in the restaurant she used to love so much. "How did you negotiate this with the property management company? I thought they were on the verge of selling?"

"I fire them," Alina said from the doorway behind them, "they were terrible."

Charlotte was numb for a moment. "Wait, Alina, *you're* my landlord?! Why did you never tell me before?"

"You're my friend," Alina said, almost shocked at the offense. "Your shop can't leave. Your woo-woo store and my nail salon is all this town has left. I told those property managers not to harass you and Faye, but they didn't listen. And that new guy across the street must have started asking them questions."

"He was probably getting the inside scoop from them about how your business had slowed," Darius added.

Charlotte nodded, "Which is why he and his realtors were calling to bug me."

The harassment and strange phone calls were all starting to make sense now, except for one thing. "But why did his realtor ask if I wanted to sell my business?"

"Because he's building condos for the young workers in the city. He knew a quirky divination and coffee shop would take off as soon as his development goes in," Darius said.

"Along with a nail salon," Alina added. "The problem was he didn't realize *I* was the landlord."

"And now we'll have a pub here," Darius added, "making our side of the street the best!" He leaned toward Charlotte and whispered in her ear, "I didn't want to tell you until it was official."

Charlotte hugged him and looked up at his strong, handsome face.

"Wait," she pulled back, "what's this about a divination and *coffee* shop?"

Darius and Alina laughed together.

Darius pulled her even closer and said "you and Faith are obsessed with coffee. You desperately need to sell it to your customers. Now that you'll have patrons waiting in the lobby for massages and tarot readings, it will be a perfect hangout spot to grab a java and buy some cool rocks."

"We can't sell coffee; we don't have a commercial kitchen."

"Look around you," Darius held his arms up and spun around in his soon-to-be pub, "all it takes is a door from your back office to my kitchen. When I signed the contract, I made sure my new landlord didn't have a problem with it."

Alina rolled her eyes and waved a disgruntled but beautifully polished hand of nails at him, "it was always going to be part of the contract," she said, "I need coffee competition for that developer guy and his weird market."

Alina left the two of them alone and headed back toward her nail salon.

Charlotte laughed, and visions of Fallstaff's future hotspot came immediately into her mind. She all but sang, "Coffee, Reiki, and fortunes in the daytime-"

"And a few shots of bad whiskey at night."

"That's going to be a long workday for me," Charlotte said, wrapping her arms around his waist.

"How about I promise to rub you down every night before bed." He leaned down and brought his lips near hers without quite touching, and whispered "You know, to get the knots out."

"I've got a type of knot you can rub out right now," she whispered, and pulled him in for a kiss.

## About the Author

Emmy Tidning lives in a magical fantasy world called the Pacific Northwest, where anything is possible, but no one is real. She has two cats, a dog, a husband, some kids, and a swarm of wasps she befriended when she saved one from drowning. Emmy reads Tarot card, writes clean romantic fun, and can be reached through the publisher at info@applieddivination.com

## Acknowledgments

This book would not be possible without:

1) Fortune teller insight from Applied Divination.
2) Paranormal women's fiction writing tips, and tons of Zoom conference calls, with author TJ Deschamps. Preorder Eastside Hedge Witch!
3) Encouragement from the Romance Writing community, the Cascade Writers organization, and the Speculative Twist Facebook group.
4) The love and support of my husband, Hoov.

## Also Published by Applied Divination

Applied Tarot
Applied Runes
Applied Tarot Reversed
Applied Divination Journal
Psychic Word Puzzles
Faye's Fortune

Visit emilypaper.com for more information.

Coming eventually from Applied Divination

# Applied Tasseography

## An Excessively Practical Guide to Interpreting Tea Leaves

What movie should you watch when a dog shows up at the bottom of your cup?

You should watch the **Truman Show!**

I will never not recommend The Truman Show.

**Follow emilypaper.com for more information!**

Coming in 2022 from Emmy Tidning

# Sloane's Solitude

Sloane has no special powers, zero magical insights, and a mental illness that keeps her homebound. When a body is discovered and her hot new neighbor is involved, will she run, or be the next victim?
**Seclude yourself with *Sloane's Solitude*, 2022**